NORMAN

A Fractured Book

SCOTT TILLEY

NORMAN

Published by

 **Unwell**

An imprint of Precious Publishing, LLC

www.PreciousPublishing.biz

ISBN-13: 978-1-951750-38-1
ISBN-13: 978-1-951750-20-6 (ebook)

TABLE OF CONTENTS

NORMAN

NORMAN

This is Norman.

You've seen him before.
At a bus stop,
in a fluorescent dream,
on a milk carton with no picture.

He's mostly functional.
He drinks tea with ghosts,
and checks his pulse against headlines.

You don't need to understand Norman.
You just need to admit you've met him.

NORMAN

Maybe it was Tuesday when you first noticed him.

Maybe he'd been there all along,
like wallpaper you finally see.

He was the person whose name you forgot mid-sentence,
the face that looked familiar until it didn't.

Norman is the space between remembering and forgetting,
the pause before you say, "never mind."

DEDICATION

For the Fractured

To anyone who's ever looked in the mirror and said, "I'm fine," with a twitching eye, a clenched jaw, and the quiet hope that no one will notice the wobble underneath.

For the Fragmented

For the ones who never had chapters, only short paragraphs. The ones who were left off the invitation but still dressed up. The ones who held their breath every time the doorbell rang.

For Norman

For what slipped through. For what hums beneath the bruise. For the parts of him that still flicker behind the static. For the face that held, even when the name didn't.

For everything I've
forgotten —

and whatever
remembered me back.

PREFACE

Norman and the art of falling apart

This book began with a face.

Not a heroic one.

Not beautiful, symmetrical,
or aspirational.

Just... Norman.

Pear-shaped, wide-eyed,
barely stitched together.

Norman came to me the way some truths do—quietly, absurdly, a little unsettling. Once seen, he was hard to ignore.

At first, I thought I was sketching a joke. Then I realized I was drawing someone I recognized—someone who flinched at light, smiled too hard, and forgot things they never meant to carry. *Someone ... not quite right. Fractured. Unwell.*

Norman is not a diagnosis. He is not a metaphor I'll explain. He's a sketch. A thread. A leak in the dam of composure.

You don't need to understand him. You only need to admit you've seen someone like him—

in a mirror,

in a hallway,

or maybe in yourself on a very dark day.

Scott Tilley
Melbourne, FL
June 13, 2025

NORMAN

ACKNOWLEDGMENTS

I created this in fragments, over time, with digital graphite on my fingers and Norman in my head. It's been a fascinating journey into the surreal. I'm not sure I've fully returned.

Thank you to a special someone who listened to me describe a quirky man with a pear-shaped head and said, "Go on."

Thank you to the musicians who provided the international soundtrack: Still Corners (UK, USA), Keep Shelley in Athens (Greece), and Arcade Fire (Canada). You were the ear candy on my bendable trip to the dystopian suburbs.

Special thanks to the hallway mirror, the crack in the wall, and the wearers of the striped shirt—I'm looking at you, Charlie, Freddy, and various jailbirds.

And, of course, thanks to the readers who lingered at the edge of the page and made space for this special kind of strange. You know who you are. Don't fall off.

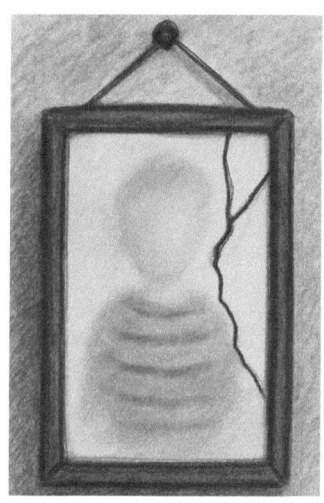

NORMAN IS FINE

Norman insists he's okay, despite the daily evidence to the contrary: lost time, twitchy eyes, echoes in his coffee. He performs fine-ness with quiet precision. At night, his teeth vibrate slightly when he smiles. He slips.

The coffee trembles.

The mirror nods.

Today hasn't noticed him yet.

Norman is fine.
He brushes his teeth. He remembers how.
He nods at the hallway mirror and the mirror nods back.
The bruise is probably from sleep.
The twitch is just static.

Norman is fine.
The alarm went off at the right time,
even though the sun didn't follow.
The toast was burnt on only one side —
that's a win.

His left shoe screamed again this morning.
But only once.
Norman is fine.

The neighbors still wave,
though one keeps mouthing "Run."
He assumes it's a joke.

His checklist is complete.
Smile. Blink. Teeth. Pants. Keys.
The order matters.
Pants before keys. Always.

He hasn't screamed into the fridge since Tuesday.
Progress.

Norman is fine.
So why is the wallpaper whispering?
And why does he smell thunderstorms in people?
And why does the doorknob pulse like a heart?

He is fine.
He is fine.
He is—
Wait. What was he saying?

THE CHECKLIST AND THE CRACK

Norman uses a checklist to keep his life together: wake up, tickle teeth, nod, smile, nod. The list grows longer each day, but so do the cracks. Some are on the walls, some in the paper. One has started whispering. He tilts.

One box unchecked.

A line on the wall that blinks.

He folds the paper wrong.

Checklist, Monday.
- ☐ Wake up.
- ☐ Verify time matches day.
- ☐ Stare into mirror. Confirm. Deny. Confirm.
- ☐ Drink water. Or at least pretend.
- ☐ Brush teeth. Don't count the clicks.

☐ Do not think about the crack.
It started as a hairline. Above the switch in the hallway.
Now it spiders across the wall,
past the mirror, into his reflection's forehead.
The crack is inside the mirror now.
It moves when he blinks.

Checklist, Tuesday.
- ☐ Wake up.
- ☐ Be upright before the fridge door creaks open.
- ☐ Ignore the voices in the floor tiles.
- ☐ Smile (forcefully).
- ☐ Keep left eye from twitching.

☐ Do not look directly at the crack.

The checklist calms Norman. Boxes are good.
Boxes are measurable. They don't lie.
The crack — well, the crack is metaphorical.
Unless it isn't.
He once touched it. It was warm.

Checklist, Wednesday.

☐ Wake up. (Barely.)

☐ Apply deodorant even if you won't see anyone.

☐ Eat something that didn't cry.

☐ Find pants. Wear them.

☐ Don't say "the crack is growing" out loud.

☐ Do not acknowledge the checklist is cracked now.

The crack hums today.
Not out loud, but like pressure behind the eyes.
Like a headache that knows your secrets.

He adds a new item at the bottom.

☐ Smile until the face holds.

☐ Breathe like no one's listening.

☐ Collapse in a manageable way.

☐ Appear functional.

☐ Appear.

☐ . . .

Norman folds the checklist in half.
It creases right down the center —
along a fresh crack.

WEARING THE WRONG FACE

Norman wears a face that doesn't belong to him. He puts it on with invisible ink every morning. It fits poorly around the eyes and makes strangers flinch. Sometimes he hears someone else's laughter coming from his mouth. In mirrors, his expression is delayed by half a second.

The smile is backwards.

His skin forgets where it ends.

The mirror shrugs again.

Norman suspects the face isn't his.

He touches his cheek and feels texture.
But when he touches his reflection, it's smooth.
He wonders: which one is lying?

He remembers looking different.
Or maybe just *feeling* different.
When his eyes didn't flinch from light.
When his teeth weren't strangers arranged in a grimace.
When smiles didn't feel borrowed.

Today's face is slightly off-center.
The left eyebrow tilts like a question.
His nostrils aren't aligned.
He pulls at his mouth, but it springs back—rubbery, eager, unfamiliar.

The face makes decisions now.
It smiles at dogs, grimaces at children, and occasionally winks at doorknobs.
Norman is just along for the ride.

He finds a note on the mirror. His own handwriting.
  "DO NOT TRUST THE EYES."

But the eyes are the only part that still look like him.
So, he erases the note, then writes a new one:
  "DO NOT TRUST THE NOTE."

Now he's confused.
But the face? The face grins wider.

He tries removing it.

First gently — ice water, lemon scrub, soft towel.
Then violently — steel wool, fingernail, duct tape.
No change.
The face clings. It wants to stay.

He leans into the mirror and whispers:
   "Whose life are you living?"

The reflection answers with a yawn.

That night, Norman falls asleep in the striped shirt.
When he wakes, the face is gone.

In its place:
   A blank surface, like frosted glass.
   No features. No history. No errors.
   Just the soft hum of something waiting to be drawn.

And the smell of lemon.

THE MAN WHO FORGOT WHY HE WAS MAD

Norman is angry. He knows that. But he's lost the cause. Was it a betrayal? A childhood wound? A headline? He types in all caps and forgets to send. He carries his rage like a lead balloon, refusing to let go, even as it deflates.

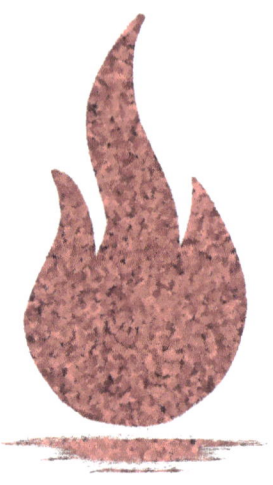

Something used to burn.

Now it hums like an unplugged lamp.

He clenches the memory anyway.

Norman was mad.

He knew that much. He felt it in the base of his skull, like an old song he didn't like but couldn't skip. Some days, it buzzed like static behind his eyes. Other days, it simmered in his teeth.

The problem was—he couldn't remember why.

It used to be something, surely. Something real. Maybe the coffee shop got his name wrong too many times. Maybe someone laughed at his shoes. Maybe the government. Or childhood. Or that look his father gave him just once. Or—

It was gone.

Now, the anger just floated. Like a helium balloon with no child attached. Bumping gently against the ceiling of his life.

At work—when he had a job—he once growled at the copy machine. A soft, gurgly growl, like something his ancestors would've made before fire. The machine jammed anyway.

In line at the pharmacy, he fantasized about shoving the man in front of him. Not out of hatred. Not even out of irritation. Just to feel gravity work on someone else for a change.

He didn't shove the man. But he clenched his jaw so hard that two of his back teeth fused. His dentist called it stress. Norman called it architecture.

Sometimes the anger took shapes. Tuesday, it was a fist in his coffee mug. Wednesday, a wasp in his shoelace. By Friday, it had spread thin like margarine across everything he touched. The doorknobs felt hostile. The sidewalk pushed back.

He kept a list of possible reasons, written in milk-colored ink on the back of an envelope:

- That thing in 1987
- The color beige

- Automatic replies
- The way people say "no worries" when clearly there are worries
- Something about teeth

But none of them fit. Like trying to unlock his apartment with a fish.

At night, the anger hummed to him in the dark. It told him he was justified. It told him to kick the fridge. It told him to scream into the carpet. But when he asked it why—why any of it—the anger would blink and shrug.

It had forgotten, too.

Norman practiced being calm. He bought a book about breathing. The book made him furious. He threw it at the wall, then apologized to the wall, then felt angry about apologizing. The cycle tasted like pennies.

Once, at a bus stop, a child screamed at him: "Why is your face like that?"

Norman didn't know which part the child meant. The twitch? The grimace? The way his forehead was eating his eyebrows?

"I'm practicing," Norman thought.

The child nodded, as if this made perfect sense.

Now, Norman carries the anger like an accessory. A stylish satchel of resentment. A hat made of fire he doesn't notice until it rains.

He tries to let it go. But he's afraid what's underneath might be worse: nothing at all.

Norman.exe Has Stopped Responding

Norman freezes mid-sentence, eyes buffering. The room continues without him. He answers questions no one asked. His pupils stutter. Somewhere deep inside, a spinning wheel turns—silent, absurd, and strangely sympathetic. He wants to believe, but his memory is fragmented. He's corrupted.

He spins.

The room buffers.

No one is holding the cord.

[SYSTEM NOTICE]

NORMAN.EXE HAS ENCOUNTERED A FATAL EXCEPTION.

Error Code: 0x1F4A (Emotional Buffer Overflow)

Suggestion: Reboot. Reframe. Resume.

Status: *Stuck in Thought Loop*

Initializing Diagnostics...

🟩 Brainstem Ping: Delayed

🟥 Emotion Handler: Crashed

🟨 Memory Recall: Fragmented
(Last Known Good Configuration: "Toaster, Tuesday")

🟩 Breathing Subroutine: Functional

🟦 Social Response AI: Outdated Patch Detected (2007)

Command Prompt > internal monologue.exe

```
>> run("basic_self_check")
```

I am Norman.

I live in a room.

The room has walls.

I think.

Or maybe I'm a process pretending to think.

Or maybe I'm the wallpaper watching someone else live me.

I feel strange.

Wait—

Feel is deprecated. Use `interpret(stimulus)` instead.

[ALERT] MEMORY OVERFLOW

"I told you already," Norman says, but no one asked anything.

He blinks twice to clear the cache. The room refreshes, but everything's in grayscale.

Even the mug. Especially the mug.

He tries to speak again.

His mouth says: "`Reinstall breakfast.`"

His brain says: "`404: Words Not Found.`"

His teeth just hum in protest.

Dialogue Fragment: Encounter with Neighbor

NEIGHBOR: Hey Norman, everything okay?

NORMAN: *...please hold... buffering...*

NEIGHBOR: You smell like wire insulation.

NORMAN: I have uploaded a smile. It may not fit.

NEIGHBOR: Alright, man. Hang in there.

[AUTOSAVE ATTEMPT FAILED]

Norman looks for a safe point.

There isn't one. Just a blinking cursor in a dark room.

The kind that asks questions and doesn't wait for the answer.

He presses escape.

Nothing happens.

The cursor blinks.

He doesn't.

The system waits.

No one answers.

Loading: `Sanity.exe` ...

Estimated time remaining: *unknown*

Corruption detected.

Restore from shadow copy? *Where is it?* **Gone.**

[END OF REPORT]

System shutting down to preserve remaining functionality.

Reboot in safe mode?

Y / N

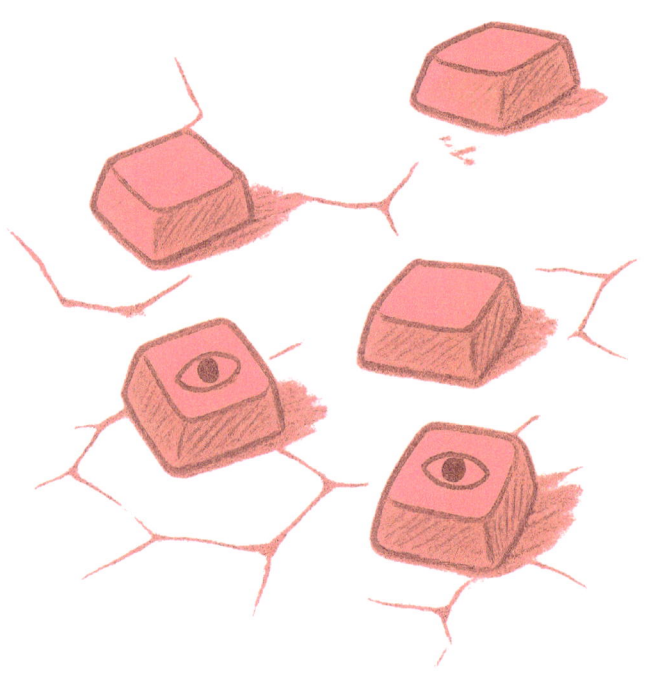

A BRUISE NAMED THURSDAY

Norman sometimes wakes with a deep violet bruise. He always names it Thursday. It's shaped like a dark thought. He doesn't know where it came from, but it giggles when he lies. As the week drags on, new bruises appear. The skin there remembers what he won't.

It pulses when he sleeps.

Whispers when he walks past glass.

He gives it a name.

Monday
Woke up with a bruise on my ribs.
Round. Soft-edged. Like a thumbprint from someone I
don't remember hugging.
Checked the mattress—no coins, no tools, no reason.
Maybe it's leftover grief.

Tuesday
Another one. Just below the collarbone.
Darker this time.
I press it and feel guilt.
Not pain—just guilt.
Did I forget something? Someone?
I wrote a sticky note: "You're not the one who bled."
No context. Not helpful.

Wednesday
They're spreading.
Left thigh. Right hip.
One shaped like a map of Michigan.
I spent ten minutes trying to find cities in it.
I think I saw Kalamazoo.

Thursday
Today's bruise has a pulse.
It rests on my forearm like it's waiting.
I named it Thursday, to keep track.
It hasn't spoken yet, but I'm listening.
It hums when I shower.
Feels warm near fluorescent lights.
Maybe it's learning me.

Friday

I didn't get a new bruise.

I missed it.

Checked my arms four times. Even used a flashlight.

Maybe this is healing.

Maybe Thursday was a friend, and I forgot to feed it.

Is that how friends work?

Saturday

There's a long one across my back.

Can't see it, but I can feel it when I lean against the wall.

The wall flinched.

So did I.

Sunday

All the bruises are gone.

But I still feel outlined.

Like someone traced me in reverse and then erased the body.

THE NORMAL GUY UNIFORM

Norman wears the same striped shirt every Monday to look "normal." But every time he puts it on, the colors look wrong. It starts smelling like burnt paper. Inside the breast pocket is a note that reads, "Don't make it weird." Eventually, the shirt begins talking to him. It's too loud to hear.

Stripes mean safety.

Stripes mean visible.

But the eyes stitched in don't blink.

Every Monday, Norman wears a polo and a strained smile.

The shirt is green with blue stripes. Faded.
It's a bit crunchy near the elbows.
He calls it the "normal guy uniform."
Because normal guys wear striped shirts. That's just a fact.
Ask any cereal box cartoon dad.

He irons it on Sundays.
Carefully. With focus. Like a ritual.
The shirt has a hole near the hem that he never fixes.
He calls it his "honesty vent."
Because normal guys have flaws, too.

When Norman wears the shirt, people seem less afraid.
Less suspicious.
As if the shirt is a permission slip to exist in public.
The barista smiles with her *whole* face.
The neighbor waves with *three fingers* instead of two.
He begins to think the shirt might be magic.

Until Thursday.

On Thursday, Norman wears the same shirt by accident.
He forgets it's not Monday.
At the corner store, a child whispers: *"Is that the man with the bruise ghost?"*

Norman drops his coins.
His teeth feel too tight in his mouth.
The cashier avoids eye contact.

The shirt is… wrong.

He rushes home.
Tears it off.
Holds it up to the light.

There are **eyes** in the fabric.
Tiny ones, stitched into the blue lines.
Blinking slowly.
Judging.

He tries to burn it.
It won't catch.
It smells like birthday cake and failure.

On Friday, Norman wears a plain grey t-shirt.
No one sees him.
Not even the mirror.

He folds the striped shirt gently.
Puts it in a box marked:
"NORMAL. DO NOT OPEN UNLESS ABSOLUTELY NECESSARY."

He tapes it shut.
He doesn't throw it away.
What if it was the only thing holding him together?

And what if next Monday comes anyway?

HOW TO BE OKAY
IN SEVEN EASY STEPS

Norman has heard about self-help courses. They have posters and smell like old success. Each step sounds helpful until it turns uncomfortable: "Step 4: Tell someone you're struggling. Then apologize." Ends with "Step 7: Forget you were ever real." The pin falls out. He begins to unravel.

He writes Step 8 in the margins.

It simply says "run."

Then he draws an off switch.

Step 1: Wake Up with Gratitude

Open your eyes and thank the universe.

Ignore the ceiling stain shaped like regret.

Do not scream into the pillow.

At least not right away.

Step 2: Hydrate and Medicate

Water is life.

Pills are personality.

Swallow both and hope for balance.

If the faucet starts whispering again, adjust your dosage.

Do not drink the second voice.

Step 3: Smile in the Mirror

Even if it cracks.

Especially if it cracks.

Count your teeth.

If the number changes, write it down.

You might need it later.

Step 4: Make Eye Contact

With a human, if possible.

With a squirrel, if necessary.

Try not to blink first.

If you do, apologize.

Then over-apologize.

Then spiral.

Step 5: Journal with Purpose

Write: "*I am fine.*"

Repeat until the pen bleeds.

Decorate with stickers of fruit.

Especially bananas.
They understand.

Step 6: Avoid the Void
Stay off news sites.
Stay out of the basement.
Stay away from mirrors after 11:11.
If a voice calls your name from under the couch, it's not your name.
Not really.

Step 7: Forgive Yourself
For being tired.
For the weird noise in your laugh.
For the unwashed forks.
For forgetting what you forgot.
For being a scribble in a world full of blueprints.

* * *

If you complete all seven steps, you'll be okay.
If not, try again tomorrow.
Unless tomorrow has teeth.
In which case:
Run sideways.
Don't look back.
Be *okay later.*

THE MIRROR ISN'T LYING, IT'S TIRED

Norman confronts his reflection. They've been fighting again. The mirror refuses to show his true face. The glass fogs, then clears, then sighs. Maybe it's just exhausted from trying. He waves sometimes, just to see if it follows. It does. But slower.

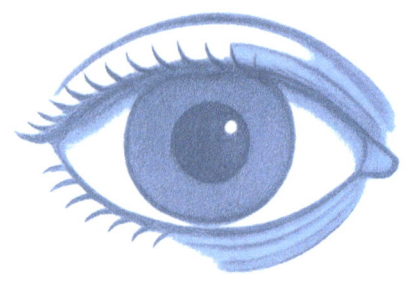

It watches kindly now.

Not with truth—just exhaustion.

He wipes it with the sleeve he cried into.

The mirror doesn't mock him anymore — it just watches.
Patient. Disappointed. Like a parent too worn to scold.

Norman stares back.
One eye twitching.
One thought stuck in a loop: *Am I still in there?*

The face in the mirror is his.
But it's grayer around the edges, more blur than bone.
It doesn't frown. It doesn't blink.
It just waits. Like it knows what's coming.

He used to ask it questions.
  "How bad is it today?"
  "Are we still pretending?"
  "What's the weather inside me?"

The mirror never answered.
But it listened. That was something.

Tonight, Norman doesn't ask.
He just exhales fog onto the glass.
Draws a smudged smiley face with a cracked finger.
It doesn't match what's underneath.

He wipes it away.
The mirror sighs.

And for the first time, Norman hears it.

PORTRAIT OF A MAN WITH A MEMORY LEAK

Norman is not fine. He begins to forget everything: names, fears, then the cracks themselves. The leaking might be a blessing—or a final erasure. He smiles. He nods. He doesn't remember why. He's fractured. He's unwell.

Something spills behind his smile.

The room forgets him softly.

But the outline still glows.

Norman forgets his alarm.
Then his keys.
Then the shape of toast.
Then the reason toast mattered.

His thoughts now slip like marbles under furniture.
He writes notes to himself:
 "You are Norman."
 "Today is real."
 "Do not pet the static."

He finds the notes the next morning.
They don't look like his handwriting.
He pockets them anyway.

The crack on the wall has sealed.
Or maybe he forgot where to look.
The mirror doesn't recognize him.
Or maybe it's just being polite.

There's a softness to the forgetting.
Like brain fog lined with fleece.
He doesn't fight it anymore.
He lets the memories drip out
and watches them stain the floor
in perfect little circles.

One day, Norman sits completely still.
The sun draws a square of light around him.
The house hums its usual off-key lullaby.
His face feels light. Hollow. Unbothered.

A small smile rises uninvited.

It doesn't belong to him, but it fits.

Later, someone finds a drawing taped to the wall.
A childlike sketch. Crooked and sweet.
A pear-headed man with a yellow bruise
and too many teeth.

It's labeled, faintly:
   "I used to be someone. He was mostly okay."

# # #

SCOTT TILLEY

Scott Tilley is an emeritus professor at the Florida Institute of Technology, president of the Center for Technology & Society, president and co-founder of Big Data Florida, president of Precious Publishing, the founding minister of CTS Ministries, and a Space Coast Writers' Guild Fellow. His recent books include *Advent Poetry* (2024), *Systems Analysis & Design* (2024), *Poems of the Moment* (2023), *AFTERMATH* (2022), and *PETS* (2021). He holds a Ph.D. in computer science from the University of Victoria. He can be reached by email at stilley@cts.today.

For more information:
- amazon.com/author/stilley
- linkedin.com/in/drtilley/
- www.CTS.today/ministries

NORMAN

 Unwell

Unwell is a boutique publishing house specializing in poetic prose exploring emotional fracture, psychological distortion, and post-apocalyptic or metaphorically devastated realities. We embrace lo-fi and anti-aesthetic design as a deliberate artistic choice, amplifying raw emotion, fractured beauty, and the imperfect human voice. Our books lean into the rough edge, the photocopied blur, the glitch in the system— because not all stories are meant to be clean.

Focusing on dark satire, uncomfortable empathy, and artistic risk, Unwell champions work that blurs the boundaries between poetry, prose, and visual art. We publish titles that resonate with readers seeking emotionally charged, stylistically daring, and beautifully unsettling experiences. Each book stands alone, but together they whisper a shared truth: we are all, in some way, unwell.

~ ~ ~

Unwell is an imprint of Precious Publishing, LLC. All our books are available online from Amazon.com, usually in print and Kindle formats. You are the author, we are the editor and publisher, and the world's biggest bookstore is the global distributor. Have an idea for a great book? Contact us!

http://www.PreciousPublishing.biz/unwell

NORMAN

👥 Fractured

Fractured is the signature series of *Unwell*, featuring a collection of slim, illustrated books that blend surreal portraiture with poetic narrative fragments. Each volume provides an intimate character study conveyed through haunting portraits, experimental text, and fractured narrative forms. With no fixed genre but a clear emotional center, these books blur the boundaries between poetry, prose, and visual storytelling.

The series explores characters unraveling at the edge of memory, identity, or perception. Through poetic monologues, malfunctioning checklists, broken dialogues, and dreamlike fragments, each book reveals a mind in crisis—sometimes comic, sometimes devastating, always deeply ... human-ish. The format is simple but precise: ten chapters, attendant images, and one persistent emotional fissure running through it all.

The first book, *Norman*, introduces a man who insists he is fine, despite all evidence to the contrary. His pear-shaped head, obsessive checklists, and cracked sense of time set the tone for what's to come. Future titles, including Agnes, Wilbur, and Ona, will continue the tradition, each figure carrying the weight of a world that's already fallen apart.

http://www.PreciousPublishing.biz/unwell

www.ingramcontent.com/pod-product-compliance
Lightning Source LLC
Chambersburg PA
CBHW041147250626
47164CB00013B/16